Meet Diego!

adapted by Leslie Valdes
based on the script by Eric Weiner
illustrated by Susan Hall

Simon Spotlight/Nick Jr.

New York   London   Toronto   Sydney   Singapore

Visit us at abdopublishing.com

Spotlight Library bound edition © 2007. Spotlight is a division of ABDO Publishing Company, Edina, Minnesota.

Simon Spotlight

An Imprint of Simon & Schuster Children's Publishing Division
1230 Avenue of the Americas, New York, New York 10020

ISBN-13 978-1-59961-243-0 (reinforced library bound edition)
ISBN-10 1-59961-243-7 (reinforced library bound edition)

Library of Congress Cataloging-In-Publication Data

This book was previously cataloged with the following information:
Valdes, Leslie
Meet Diego! / adapted by Leslie Valdes ; based on the script by Eric Weiner; illustrated by Susan Hall.
p. cm -- (Dora the Explorer ; #4)
ISBN 0-689-85993-7
Summary: Join Dora and her cousin Diego at the Animal Rescue Center, where they embark on an expedition to save Baby Jaguar from plunging over a waterfall.
[1. Dora the explorer (Fictitious character)--Juvenile fiction. 2. Animal rescue--Juvenile fiction. 3. Cousins--Juvenile fiction. 4. Dora the explorer (Fictitious character)--Fiction. 5. Animal rescue--Fiction. 6. Cousins--Fiction.] I. TItle. II. Series: Dora the Explorer ; #4.

[Fic]--dc22   2004272377

All Spotlight books are reinforced library binding and
manufactured in the United States of America.

¡Hola! I'm Dora, and this is my friend, Boots. We're at the Animal Rescue Center, where they help all kinds of animals.

Eeep, eeep!

Errr, errr!

I hear a sound. Look—Baby Bear is about to fall out of the tree! Hang on, Baby Bear! Oh, no—he's falling!

Meow, meow!

Here comes my cousin, Diego. He's saving Baby Bear. Wow!
Diego's really cool. He can make animal noises and talk to wild
animals.

Can you say "Errrr, errrr!" to Baby Bear?

Uh-oh! Someone's calling for help. Diego's field journal helps him identify animals. Let's check it to figure out who's calling for help.

It's Baby Jaguar, and he's in trouble! We've got to get to the waterfall to help him!

Map says that to get to Baby Jaguar we need to go through the rain forest and past the cave, and that's how we'll get to the waterfall. Will you help us save Baby Jaguar? We have to hurry! *¡Vámonos!*

We made it to the rain forest! Look—there's a zip cord!
We can ride the zip cord through the treetops and zip through
the rain forest.

Do *you* see a ladder we can climb up?
Oh, no! The ladder is missing six rungs. Let's find the rungs.

Thanks for helping fix the ladder. Now let's go save Baby Jaguar. Wheee!

We made it to the cave! Do you see a polar bear?
Diego's journal says polar bears live only in the cold. But it's really, really hot in the rain forest. . . .

Oh, no! That's not a polar bear! Do you know who it is? It's Swiper, that sneaky fox. He'll try to swipe Diego's journal. We have to say "Swiper, no swiping!" Say it with me: "Swiper, no swiping!"

Thanks for helping us stop Swiper! Now we need to find the waterfall. We can use Diego's spotting scope to see things that are far away!

There's the waterfall. . . . And there's Baby Jaguar!
We're coming, Baby Jaguar!

We can water-ski down the river to save Baby Jaguar.
Diego says if we ask the dolphin, he'll pull us through the water.
Can you help me call the dolphin? Say "Click, click!" Again!

Click, click!

The dolphin can pull us through the river, but we need
something to hold on to. Let's check Backpack! Say "Backpack!"
What can the dolphin use to pull us along the water?

A rope! *¡Excelente!* We all need to hold on to the rope. Put your hands out in front of you and hold on tight. Whoaaaa!

Yeah! We made it to the other side of the river.
Oh, no! Baby Jaguar is about to fall over the giant waterfall!
Diego says the big condors can help us: They can fly us all the way
to Baby Jaguar. Say "Squawk, squawk!" to call the big condors!

Squawk, squawk!

Quick! You have to help us fly to Baby Jaguar!
Flap your arms. Faster!

Hooray! We caught him!

We saved Baby Jaguar, and now the whole Jaguar family is together again. Thanks for helping!